Acting Edition

I Need That

by Theresa Rebeck

FOR PRODUCTION INQUIRIES

UNITED STATES AND CANADA
info@concordtheatricals.com
1-866-979-0447

UNITED KINGDOM AND EUROPE
licensing@concordtheatricals.co.uk
020-7054-7298

Each title is subject to availability from Concord Theatricals Corp., depending upon country of performance. Please be aware that *I NEED THAT* may not be licensed by Concord Theatricals Corp. in your territory. Professional and amateur producers should contact the nearest Concord Theatricals Corp. office or licensing partner to verify availability.

No one shall make any changes in this title(s) for the purpose of production. No part of this book may be reproduced, stored in a retrieval system, scanned, uploaded, or transmitted in any form, by any means, now known or yet to be invented, including mechanical, electronic, digital, photocopying, recording, videotaping, or otherwise, without the prior written permission of the publisher. No one shall share this title(s), or any part of this title(s), through any social media or file hosting websites.

For all inquiries regarding motion picture, television, online/digital and other media rights, please contact Concord Theatricals Corp.

MUSIC AND THIRD-PARTY MATERIALS USE NOTE

Licensees are solely responsible for obtaining formal written permission from copyright owners to use copyrighted music and/or other copyrighted third-party materials (e.g. artworks, logos) in the performance of this play and are strongly cautioned to do so. If no such permission is obtained by the licensee, then the licensee must use only original music and materials that the licensee owns and controls. Licensees are solely responsible and liable for clearances of all third-party copyrighted materials, including without limitation music, and shall indemnify the copyright owners of the play(s) and their licensing agent, Concord Theatricals Corp., against any costs, expenses, losses and liabilities arising from the use of such copyrighted third-party materials by licensees. For music, please contact the appropriate music licensing authority in your territory for the rights to any incidental music.

IMPORTANT BILLING AND CREDIT REQUIREMENTS

If you have obtained performance rights to this title, please refer to your licensing agreement for important billing and credit requirements.

I NEED THAT was commissioned and originally produced by Roundabout Theater Company in New York City, and premiered on October 13th, 2023. The performance was directed by Moritz von Stuelpnagel, with sets by Alexander Dodge, costumes by Tilly Grimes, lighting design by Yi Zhao, sound design by Fitz Patton and Bradlee Ward, hair and makeup design by Tommy Kurzman, and original music by Fitz Patton. The Production Stage Manager was Jereme Kyle Lewis. The cast was as follows:

SAM . . . . Danny DeVito

FOSTER . . . . Ray Anthony Thomas

AMELIA . . . . Lucy DeVito

CHARACTERS

SAM – Any ethnicity, late 70s/early 80s. A vital, intelligent, funny guy, a raconteur who won't give up the chaos of all the stuff he has, which is everywhere.

FOSTER – Black, late 70s, Sam's best friend. Easygoing, working class. Enjoys Sam's eccentricies. There is real love between them.

AMELIA – Any ethnicity, mid/late 30s, Sam's daughter, harried but strong. Adores her father as much as she is frustrated by him.

SETTING

Sam's house, which is cluttered with an intense level of stuff.
It's just this side of a hoarder's disaster area.

TIME

The present.

AUTHOR'S NOTES

The description of the couch can be altered to reflect the couch that is on the set.

It's important to find the balance between the dire situation Sam is in, and not letting the clutter on the set go too far. He is not crazy. But there should be no question that he has way too much stuff.

(The kitchen and living room of a decent-sized house, once well-kept, now fallen into disarray.)

(The place is an astonishing vision of stuff. Some things are wonderful, but there are lots of piles of papers and old magazines as well. It seems just like a complete disaster, but there is also beauty in there. At moments it's possible that someone lavished love on the placement of a chair next to a plant. But that impulse to organize was in the distant past.)

(This is not a hoarder's space, but it is only a few steps away from it.)

*(**SAM** enters, ready for bed, and gets into his barcolounger in the middle of this mess. After he settles in, he claps his hands twice and the light by the side of the chair goes off. He settles in to sleep.)*

(The lights shift. It is the following morning.)

(The sound of knocking. Then more knocking. Then banging.)

*(**SAM** wakes up.)*

SAM. Yeah yeah yeah hold your horses. I'm coming I'm coming.

What time is it? It's two in the morning. What do you want, it's two in the morning. Stop hammering on my door.

FOSTER. *(Offstage.)* Hey SAM.

SAM. Where's the door. Hang on, I don't know where the door is. I can't find the door, can you knock a few more times so I know where I'm going? Okay okay okay

(The knocking starts up again.)

Where am I?

*(He finds the door and opens it. **FOSTER** enters, carrying a paper bag.)*

WHOA.

(He is caught in the blast of light.)

What is that, the sun? What the hell it's two in the morning!

(He shuts the door fast.)

FOSTER. It's two in the afternoon.

SAM. No.

FOSTER. Yeah, man. You just got out of bed?

*(**FOSTER** turns on lights and opens blinds, also claps his hands. The light next to Sam's chair goes on.)*

SAM. I took three ambien. Wow. That shit works. You want a coffee?

FOSTER. I won't say no. I was down at the croissant place, got you that ham and cheese croissant, I know you like those.

SAM. You're the one who likes the ham and cheese.

FOSTER. Am I? You know what? I am!

(He laughs, and takes it.)

SAM. What else you got in there.

(*He goes to make coffee, while* **FOSTER** *clears off a place on the couch for him to sit.*)

FOSTER. Chocolate. Spinach. Almond. Two plains. I like a plain croissant too. You heat 'em up a little and put some butter and jelly on them, delicious.

SAM. You got enough croissant for half of America.

FOSTER. The day old stuff, they're practically giving them away down there. They're still good. You don't want 'em I can take them home with me.

SAM. I didn't say I didn't want 'em.

FOSTER. It sounds like you don't want 'em.

SAM. Well give me a chance I'm just waking up.

FOSTER. What are you doing.

SAM. I'm getting a glass of water.

FOSTER. What for?

SAM. That's what they say now, you're supposed to be drinking water all the time. First thing in the morning, you have to have a glass of water.

FOSTER. Who says that?

SAM. Listen I'm just repeating something that was given to me as a useful piece of I don't know.

(*He has a bottle of water in his hand.*)

FOSTER. You buying water in bottles now?

SAM. What? No, I refill this. I bought this in Calabasas in 1976. The water comes out of the sink.

FOSTER. Good. That makes no sense to me, water in bottles. Just never did. Plants in the earth do just fine with water out of the sky. Good enough for them.

SAM. How's your garden these days?

FOSTER. You should see it. It's crazy, things growing everywhere. I put in a couple of those plants they're just a giant leaf. Like a leaf this big. Then I got those vines I put in a couple years ago, they're everywhere now. And I got this giant oak leaf hydrangea, cost me fifteen dollars last year, it's the size of I don't know what. It's big, it likes it out there. So green and leafy, big white flowers. That Mrs. Gundersun, she never had nothing out there, it was like a little square of dry earth. Now she wants to charge me more because I made the place so nice.

SAM. Predictable.

FOSTER. Right? Anyway it's nice out there, everything growing. Not everything. Some things are dying already, some of them don't last long, you got to be sure to get out there and pull them up or they take up too much room when all they're doing is dying.

SAM. Sounds like you and me.

(They laugh.)

Don't touch that. Hey. Don't touch that.

*(For **FOSTER** is now moving things around so that he can spread out the croissants.)*

FOSTER. I got to put them somewhere.

SAM. I got things the way I like it over there. And don't sit there, neither.

FOSTER. It's the only place to sit!

SAM. There's plenty of places to sit. Sit there.

(He points. Goes back to the kitchen.)

FOSTER. You got to clean this place up, Sam.

SAM. I'm doing it. You know, I'm organizing.

FOSTER. You need to organize some of this right out the door. Ow. What's this.

> (*He sits and then stands up. He holds something in his hand.*)

SAM. You sit on that? Don't sit on that. I need that. You can't just sit wherever you want, you know.

FOSTER. It's a bottle cap.

SAM. That's right it's a bottle cap. It's sixty-seven years old. It's worth something.

FOSTER. Sixty-seven-year-old bottle cap isn't worth anything.

SAM. That's what you think. That's from my youth. Okay. When I was a kid I used to sell sodas at Our Lady of Mount Carmel Bingo, every Friday night. Grape Fanta, Pepsi, that kind of Jamaican lemon lime. They'd bring this big block of ice by the bingo hall and I'd chop it up to put the bottles in it, keep 'em cold. All night people are yelling at me, bring me a soda! SAMMY! Bring me a soda! The place was always packed. Father John up there calling out the numbers, it was crazy. Those little plastic chips, I got some of those around here too.

FOSTER. You saved the bingo chips.

SAM. The priest used to make me pick 'em up and put them in those little glassine bags, twelve to a bag, they'd resell 'em for a dime. They're here somewhere. Here it is, here it is.

> (*He shows him a box with stuff in it.* **FOSTER** *looks through it.*)

FOSTER. This all come from Bingo night?

SAM. Our Lady of Mount Carmel Bingo. Every Friday night. I'd come home smelling like a chimney. Everybody smoked like two to three packs a night. The place was like a giant diseased lung. It was a wild time.

FOSTER. What's this?

SAM. That's a ring.

FOSTER. Looks like an engagement ring.

SAM. Yeah the ladies sometimes took their rings off, somehow it made it easier to play bingo, I'm not sure why. Their hands got sweaty, I think, so if the ring was loose you took it off. Or if it was tight maybe, all that sweat provided an opportunity.

FOSTER. So this person left their wedding ring on the table, while she was playing bingo and then what, it fell on the floor and you found it in there with the garbage?

SAM. That's right.

FOSTER. This is a real engagement ring? This is a real diamond? And you didn't turn it in to the priest?

SAM. Oh what's he going to do with it. He's going to put it in the collection plate. Because the Pope needs another ring.

FOSTER. It's pretty. It's probably worth something.

SAM. Everything here is worth something.

FOSTER. You say that Sam but I think this might actually be worth something.

SAM. Hey don't just eat that without a plate, you slob. You get crumbs everywhere. Here, let me get you a plate.

FOSTER. You could sell this.

SAM. You want me to sell some old lady's wedding ring?

FOSTER. She's an old lady?

SAM. They were all old ladies! They were playing bingo on Friday night! And this was sixty years ago. She's dead. Even if I wanted, I couldn't return it.

FOSTER. Poor thing. She lost her wedding ring, at bingo night.

(He considers the ring, tosses it back in the box with the bingo chips.)

SAM. She was not a nice person.

FOSTER. You knew her?

SAM. None of them were all that nice. A couple of 'em would give me a buck if they hit the bingo. The rest of them, these were hardened women. The hairstyles were very threatening, huge, like helmets. They came to play but they weren't playing around, you know what I mean? Their fingernails, you can imagine. Sharp as a blade and blood red, all of them. The stiletto shoes. These women were not victims. I need some jam.

(He heads for the kitchen.)

FOSTER. *(Considering the box.)* How come you saved the chips but not the cards?

SAM. They aren't in there? I don't know where they went. Ginny must've moved them at some point. She's gone three years, I'm still trying to figure out where things are.

(Knocks on the door. More knocks.)

What the hell, it's Grand Central Station today.

*(**FOSTER** looks through the blinds.)*

FOSTER. Oh, it's Amelia.

SAM. What, Amelia? You didn't tell me it was Amelia. Do not open the door.

(He goes and starts to move a pile of magazines and blankets. It is not clear immediately where he is moving it.)

FOSTER. Why not?

SAM. I didn't know she was coming today.

AMELIA. *(Offstage.)* Hey Dad, I know you're in there.

> (**SAM** *continues to clean with no apparent effect.*)

SAM. *(Calling.)* I didn't know you were coming today, honey! I can't come to the door.

FOSTER. What do you want me to do? I'm going to open the door.

AMELIA. Mr. Foster? I can hear you in there.

SAM. It's not, it's not a good time!

AMELIA. Mr. Foster, can you open the door for me?

SAM. Tell her to go away.

FOSTER. I'm not going to tell her that.

AMELIA. *(Offstage.)* I can hear you both talking in there, I know you're there, open the door.

> (**SAM** *moves things around.*)

SAM. *(Overlap.)* I just got up. I'm naked. I don't want you coming in here and seeing me naked.

AMELIA. *(Overlap.)* OPEN THE DOOR. DAD. You are not naked! I know you are not naked!

> (**SAM** *continues to move things around.*)

SAM. No. Wait. Okay. Okay, you can let her in. Let her in. Yes, it's fine, let her in.

> (**FOSTER** *opens the door.* **AMELIA** *enters. She is lovely and fierce and pragmatic. She has a bag full of groceries.*)

AMELIA. Thank you Mr. Foster.

FOSTER. Hey Amelia. You look good.

AMELIA. Thank you!

FOSTER. Makeup on, your hair looks so nice.

AMELIA. I got a job interview this afternoon. Hi Daddy.

(*She hands the bag to* **SAM**.)

SAM. What's this?

AMELIA. Groceries. Here's some broccoli, it's already chopped up so you just have to steam it, butternut squash also already chopped, you bake this, in the oven, carrots, some apples and – tada! Lettuce.

SAM. Oh like vegetables.

AMELIA. Yes Dad you should be eating vegetables, we talked about this.

SAM. This looks great honey. Thanks. Let me find a place.

AMELIA. The refrigerator is a place.

SAM. That's a great idea. I'll put this in the refrigerator. This looks great. Eating my vegetables, drinking my water. Drinking a lot of water, like you told me. I mean, some people might think, you get to a certain age, you can eat and drink whatever you want.

AMELIA. Who thinks that?

SAM. Nobody.

(**SAM** *starts to put the vegetables away.*)

AMELIA. (*Looking around.*) So the place looks – worse. It just looks worse!

SAM. Look, I've been organizing. I've been moving things around. You know how that is. You're in the middle of cleaning, and suddenly everything looks worse? That's what's happening.

AMELIA. I see that that *happened*, you moved things around –

(She picks up a few pieces of clothing to show him.)

SAM. Those are your mother's clothes.

(He takes them from her. She remains frustrated.)

AMELIA. You finally brought her stuff down from upstairs, piled it all on top of everything else that was already here, made everything worse, and then you stopped. Isn't that what happened? That's what happened.

SAM. *(Irritated.)* This is my process.

AMELIA. This is not PROCESS.

SAM. You can't just throw out everything. You have to figure out what you want to keep, and what you can let go. It's like *Sophie's Choice.*

AMELIA. *(Really frustrated.)* This is not like *SOPHIE'S CHOICE*! This is like: The fire department is coming and they're going to condemn the place and tell the health department to throw you out if you don't do something.

This is a disaster. This is collapse. The weight of the universe –

SAM. Here she goes.

AMELIA. Not the universe, yes, the universe, a black hole, sucking itself and everything around it into – gravity pulling everything into entropy – You know what this is? This is not *Sophie's Choice,* this is *Carrie,* the end of *Carrie.* Where the house is so full of terrible things it just sucks itself into the earth. And poor psycho Carrie and her evil mother are buried, just completely buried. Under the wreckage. Of their lives. That's what this is. And that is what is going to happen to you.

SAM. Okay look. I get it, I get what you're saying, but I'm not a burden on anyone. Am I a burden? I own my house. I have my money in the pension, I live within my means. I don't know why this bothers you so much. So I don't mow my lawn, it has weeds in it. Who cares?

I'm telling both of you. I'm a solid citizen. I'm not making problems. I'm not making people suffer.

AMELIA. You're making me suffer. This is an incredible headache that I have been dealing with –

SAM. I don't even go outside! I stay in my house, with my things.

AMELIA. No, you stay in here with your head in the sand!

SAM. I'm an American. It's my right. I don't bother them, why should they bother me –

AMELIA. Well, you're going to LOSE your rights because they asked you to take care of your yard. They didn't even ask you, they told you! Several times! For EIGHT MONTHS!

FOSTER. This has been going on for eight months?

AMELIA. I know! I know! He's been hiding it from me for seven! And all he had to do was have someone come cut his grass. There's a guy on the internet who does

SAM. They can't make me cut my grass.

AMELIA. But they can call the fire department.

SAM. They can't take my house because I don't cut the grass!

FOSTER. I want to talk to that guy who will cut that grass for free.

AMELIA. He was here! He was going to do it! Dad screamed at him until he left!

SAM. That's very special indigenous grass out there.

AMELIA. It's weeds –

SAM. It's a nature preserve, it's an ecosystem with grasshoppers, and birds who come and eat them and the bees and the butterflies pollinate the flowers.

FOSTER. What did the fire department say?

SAM. Who cares.

AMELIA. I care. How about you, Mr. Foster, do you care?

FOSTER. I kind of do.

AMELIA. Where are the letters? There were like ten letters. They were right here!

(She starts to look.)

FOSTER. Sam, you didn't tell me anything about this. You got letters?

SAM. Form letters.

AMELIA. The last three were not form letters! They had the green things stuck to the back of them, they were certified and you sat on all of them for weeks before you alerted me!

FOSTER. Can I see one?

SAM. I don't know where they are.

AMELIA. He's been hiding them.

SAM. I didn't hide them, I just didn't look at them.

AMELIA. I looked at them. Once you showed them to me. And I called the fire department and there's this thing called "code enforcement" and while they can't just throw you out without cause –

SAM. That's what I mean.

AMELIA. You gave them cause to inspect it! That lady across the street has pictures! She snuck over here and took pictures through the windows. She's got it all. In all its glory. She sent them in and made a complaint. And the health department is allowed to come and throw you out if the fire department shows up and says you're a danger to yourself.

FOSTER. That's a lot of steps.

SAM. That's what I say. It's going to take them forever. The way these assholes work, everything takes –

AMELIA. Not anymore! Forever is behind us. The fire department is next week. NEXT WEEK.

FOSTER. Why didn't you tell me about this?

SAM. Because it's stupid! That Mrs. Wallace, across the street –

AMELIA. That is her name.

SAM. She's an unpleasant woman. And she just came up on my porch and took pictures through the window.

FOSTER. She took pictures?

SAM. You're in some of them.

FOSTER. How do I look?

SAM. Good, you look good. These photos are very slimming.

FOSTER. No, I been working out.

(*They laugh.*)

AMELIA. Guys, this actually not funny –

FOSTER. I know, I know. Could he sue her for that?

AMELIA. Sure he can sue her from the Public Library which is where he will be living.

FOSTER. You should call a lawyer, Sam.

SAM. Everybody's favorite food group.

AMELIA. I've talked to a lawyer. This is what she told me. You have to make a good faith effort. Otherwise they can in fact condemn this place and take you out and put you in state housing.

SAM. Oh come on. This is America.

AMELIA. Yes and sometimes they actually enforce a few of the laws, not a lot of them, but they seem especially keen about bothering old men who are living alone and posing a danger to themselves.

SAM. A danger? How am I a danger? I mean, I don't have any guns in here.

AMELIA. This is not a good faith effort.

SAM. Sure it is.

AMELIA. Dad, a good faith effort has a lot of different definitions, but doing nothing is not one of them.

FOSTER. Can I see the letters?

SAM. I threw 'em away.

AMELIA. Oh THAT you throw away. You can't throw away a single thing from thirty years ago but the one thing we need –

FOSTER. Wait wait wait. Here it is! Least here's one of them.

(*He's found it.*)

SAM. There it is. I didn't throw it away.

AMELIA. Okay. Thank you Mr. Foster. Maybe you can get him to read it and he can see that I'm not making this up. Wait. Let me take a picture of it so that we don't lose it, again.

(*She does.* **FOSTER** *tries to help.*)

FOSTER. My sense is he's not going out and buying more stuff, if you're worried about that. He's not doing that.

AMELIA. I don't think that counts as "good faith."

FOSTER. I'm just saying you're not here as often because of your work but I do come over and spend time here and seriously it's not like that show.

SAM. What show?

FOSTER. The one on TV about the –

(He stops himself. He doesn't want to say it.)

SAM. What's it about?

AMELIA. Hoarders! It's about crazy people who hoard everything because they're insane and the whole universe collapses around them, it was on TV for like a hundred years.

SAM. I don't know anything about that.

AMELIA. Because you don't have a TV and you don't have a clue anymore about how the world actually works.

FOSTER. It doesn't matter because this is nothing like that.

AMELIA. *(Firm.)* Mr. Foster thank you, thank you for everything you do for him, but please do not enable him around this. It makes everything harder.

FOSTER. Okay.

SAM. "Enable." "Enable." I hate that word. "Enable."

AMELIA. How about this word: Eviction. Here's another one. Homeless. Dying on the street. You like any of those words?

SAM. Amelia. Listen. I don't need you to come over here and tell me that you're unhappy with the way I live. I live the way I live. If you don't like it, you don't have to come.

FOSTER. Oh come on she just got here. She's got to stay for a minute, at least! You want a croissant, Amelia? I brought over these croissants.

AMELIA. I don't want a croissant. I'm trying to lose weight.

FOSTER. You don't need to lose weight. You're beautiful. Sam, tell her how pretty she looks.

SAM. You do, you look very nice.

(A sad pause.)

FOSTER. You got a job interview?

AMELIA. Yes.

FOSTER. Something wrong with the old job? You always said you liked that job.

AMELIA. They restructured. I mean they had things they wanted me to do. It just, none of them were a good fit.

FOSTER. I bet they're sorry to see you go.

AMELIA. Yes. They are.

(Another pause.)

Can I have chocolate? Do you have almond?

FOSTER. I got whatever you want, honey.

AMELIA. Could I have a carrot?

FOSTER. If that's what you want.

AMELIA. I brought some carrots, in the, with the –

FOSTER. The vegetables?

AMELIA. I'll just have a croissant.

FOSTER. Great. 'Cause we got plenty. When they have day old stuff at the bakery, it's a real good deal.

AMELIA. There's no place to sit.

FOSTER. Here on the couch is a good place. Is it okay if I move some stuff?

SAM. I don't, sitting on the couch is not, seriously you can't sit there.

(She nods, accepting that.)

FOSTER. But this idea. About getting some of this out of here, letting the neighbors see that you're acknowledging their concern, that's a good idea, Sam. I could come over this weekend and help you with that.

AMELIA. That's a great idea, Mr. Foster. I brought over all these garbage bags last week. If you could even just help him fill up some garbage bags, it would be great.

FOSTER. I can do that.

AMELIA. Thank you.

SAM. Okay just

AMELIA. No just. No just!

SAM. Look. I said I'd do it. And I am doing it. I'm organizing, I'm being selective. It just might take me a little longer than the "weekend."

AMELIA. Dad.

SAM. "Garbage" is not – if you think this is "garbage" –

AMELIA. What?

SAM. You said garbage bags.

AMELIA. Yeah –

SAM. And it's just, if you think of it as garbage, if that's how you come at it from the jump then you're not going to know how to organize it. You have to see that that's true. I mean, you think that all of this is garbage when none of it is garbage. So you're not the best person to explain to me how to organize.

*(**AMELIA** nods. Pause.)*

AMELIA. Could someone hold this for me?

(She holds out the croissant.)

FOSTER. You don't want it?

AMELIA. I can't eat it! There's no place to set it down!

> (**FOSTER** *takes the stuff.* **SAM** *starts to move things.)*

SAM. Well here, here.

AMELIA. Stop. Stop. I have to. Sorry. I have to go be ready for my, I have to go. Goodbye.

Mr. Foster. Goodbye Dad.

> *(She shakes her head, climbs back over the piles of stuff, and goes. The* **MEN** *watch her.)*

FOSTER. She's a good girl.

SAM. A little high-strung.

FOSTER. I'll go put this back in the kitchen.

SAM. I'll do it.

> *(He takes the dishes from* **FOSTER**. **FOSTER** *watches him go. When* **SAM***'s back is turned, he goes to the box with the ring in it, takes the ring, puts the box back where it was, then goes back to the door.)*

(Offstage, in kitchen.) My kitchen is spotless, why doesn't that count? You should see my cleaning materials, under the sink. I have a toothbrush to clean the grout in the tiles in here. Why doesn't that count. I have a lot of dishes in here that's true but they're all clean. The dishwasher does a good job. Why doesn't that count. The bathroom, spotless! I got my own washer/dryer. Why doesn't that count.

> (**FOSTER** *has kept a keen eye on his whereabouts so that* **SAM** *doesn't see what he's done. Now he edges toward the door.)*

FOSTER. I'm going to take off now.

SAM. Oh yeah?

FOSTER. Yeah, I got some errands to run, gonna see if they have a sale down at the garden store. Sometimes they're just getting rid of stuff, you can get a good deal.

SAM. That sounds

FOSTER. Okay.

(*He starts to go.*)

SAM. Hey Foster.

FOSTER. Yeah.

(*He's itching to go now. But* **SAM** *is there, talking to him.*)

SAM. There's a program? About other people, who live like, they like keeping their stuff.

FOSTER. Some of them go too far. You know they leave garbage on the floor, cats, like I said, rodents even, I saw one where a guy had rats everywhere.

SAM. (*Disturbed.*) Rats. That's horrendous.

FOSTER. They pick up piles of stuff, there's dead things under there. It's extreme.

SAM. Dead things? That has to smell.

FOSTER. Apparently it does.

SAM. I'm not like that.

FOSTER. No no no. This isn't anything like that.

SAM. Rats?

FOSTER. I'm telling you, it's not you. You change your clothes every day, you clean the kitchen, the bathroom, like you said.

SAM. I do all that.

FOSTER. Yeah, the lady across the street is a nuisance and the government is sticking its nose in, that's your real problem. These people on the television show, they're lost souls.

SAM. I'm not a lost soul.

FOSTER. That's what I'm saying.

(Lights fade. **FOSTER** *leaves.)*

Scene Two

(**SAM** *alone, at night. He wanders, restless, considers the mess for a moment, then finally reaches back into the upper levels of junk, and pulls out something rather large. He pulls it out. It is an old television set. An old one. Maybe from the sixties.*)

(*He looks at the priceless treasure he has recovered. He takes it over to the wall by the kitchen and sets it on the pile of magazines, realizes that will not be big enough.*)

(*He turns on the television. Static comes on. He thinks about that.*)

(*Then he brings the television down a little bit, balances it on a lower pile of papers, and pulls out the rabbit ears. Static. He plays with the rabbit ears. More static.*)

(*Then suddenly, the television lights on an old show, a song, from an old game show. Possibly* Jeopardy, *or something like that.*[*] *The theme song is loud and clear.*)

(*Delighted,* **SAM** *watches for a moment. Then the static returns.* **SAM** *tries to move the rabbit ears again. The music and lights*

---

[*] A license to produce *I Need That* does not include a performance license for "Think!" (The *Jeopardy!* theme song). The publisher and author suggest that the licensee contact ASCAP or BMI to ascertain the music publisher and contact such music publisher to license or acquire permission for performance of the song. If a license or permission is unattainable for "Think!", the licensee may not use the song in *I Need That* but should create an original composition in a similar style or use a similar song in the public domain. For further information, please see the Music and Third-Party Materials Use Note on page iii.

return! But he taps the television just to make sure it stays on. And then the static returns, sparks and smoke! **SAM** *waves the smoke away with a magazine. Blackout.)*

Scene Three

(Two days later. **AMELIA** *is there, looking at the television.* **SAM** *is alight with excitement.* **FOSTER** *comes out of the kitchen, with a cup of coffee.)*

SAM. It's from the sixties! The nineteen sixties.

AMELIA. And it still works?

SAM. It worked! For like thirty seconds, it worked.

FOSTER. Looks like a time machine.

SAM. It's exactly like a time machine. You know what I tuned in to? *Jeopardy.*[*] Seriously. It played the music from *Jeopardy*, like straight out of the past. And then it stopped.

AMELIA. Well –

SAM. It happened!

AMELIA. Yeah but it wasn't from the past, Dad, it was from the present.

SAM. No no it was that show from when we were kids. Where they give you the answer and you ask the question.

FOSTER. That show is still on, she means.

SAM. What?

FOSTER. That show. Is on now. You didn't like – pipe it in from the past.

SAM. Yeah but it's like the same show, like literally. The blue squares and the

---

* If licensees are unable to obtain performance rights for "Think!", they can replace this dialogue to match the game show and theme song for which they obtain performance rights.

FOSTER. Oh yeah

SAM. And the same song, I mean the song is exactly the same.

(*Sings.*)

DO DO DO DO DO DO DO.

DO DO DO DO DOO.

DOO DOO DOO DO DO

DO DO DO DO

(**FOSTER** *chimes in. They sing the song together.*)

(*And then* **AMELIA** *joins in. They sing the rest of the song. They laugh.*)

FOSTER. Oh yeah yeah sorry I thought

SAM. Wait wait wait. What did you think I literally thought this television was picking up radio waves from sixty years ago?

FOSTER. I didn't know, it sounded

SAM. What do you think I'm nuts or something?

(*They laugh at this.*)

Look at this; look at this.

(*He takes the case of the television right off of it.*)

FOSTER. Whoa, that thing is falling apart.

SAM. No no no, this is how it was. My dad made this.

FOSTER. Come on.

(*As he takes the television apart, he narrates.*)

SAM. We had no money. Like none. My parents kept having kids they couldn't afford, it was a pretty typical story, I can't even remember how many brothers and sisters I got. Like nine. Eight. Like I said I can't remember.

AMELIA. You have five sisters and two brothers.

SAM. What she said. I can't remember their names.

AMELIA. Lucy, Paul, Jenny, Robert –

SAM. Most them, as I recall, were not all that nice. Well why would they be, I was like this little kid and they were, I was like a football to them, just something to kick around the backyard. Catholic families. You got to ask. The girls were better than the boys. Anyway there comes a point when they're all agitating for a television set. Not just any television set: A color television set. Because we had one, black and white, when you watched *The Wizard of Oz* it was meaningless. And my parents couldn't afford a color TV. They could barely afford to feed us! So no color television.

> *(He thinks about this for a moment, shakes his head.)*

My dad he's working down at a garage fixing cars, my mom is at home drowning in children, so there's universal agitation about this color television set but no chance, really, that the situation is going to improve. And then one day my dad comes home from the garage with this huge box. Several boxes. And he takes them into the family room, it was this old porch that he had walled in at some point so there's no heat out there, it's not comfortable, and he starts to unpack these boxes.

FOSTER. And it was a TV set.

SAM. It was a kit, to build a TV set.

AMELIA. I never heard this story.

FOSTER. Me neither.

> *(It is more and more interesting to them.* **AMELIA** *settles in to listen while* **FOSTER** *investigates the TV.)*

SAM. You could buy these kits. And they sent instructions with all the tubes, like these right here, with the tungsten and wires and screws and bolts and washers and you needed a soldering iron, one of those old things that would shoot lead out, and melt it and you solder everything in place, it smelled terrible.

FOSTER. Hang on.

SAM. So he spread all this stuff out, on this old card table in the family room.

FOSTER. Which had no heat.

SAM. It had some heat, just not a lot. No insulation. So he spread all this stuff out on the table and every night when he came home he'd go out there and work on building this television. And we'd all stand around and watch. It was fantastic. He was like a magician, with that soldering iron. All these kids surrounding him and watching that thing light up.

SAM. And then one day we had a color TV. It never worked very well. Television. What a disappointment.

FOSTER. I don't know. At night, it's nice, you have a television set, you're not alone. Watch the news. The whole world is with you.

SAM. Be real. It's you and a little box, got some lights. Every now and then it plays the song to some gameshow.

FOSTER. It does more than that.

SAM. Yeah but you're still alone. You live in that apartment alone, alone with a TV.

FOSTER. That is depressing.

AMELIA. So this can go. I mean, we should take this to an antique store. I've got a bunch of bubble wrap in the car, let's wrap it up and take it downtown, there's a couple places I think would love it.

SAM. Oh right now?

AMELIA. Absolutely. The clock is ticking. Let me go get the bubble wrap.

(*She goes.* **FOSTER** *looks at* **SAM.**)

SAM. Bubble wrap. In the car. She's always got packing materials. She travels with them.

(*He takes the television and hides it back in all the junk somewhere while they talk.*)

FOSTER. That's a good thing.

SAM. Come on. I just got played. By my own kid.

FOSTER. Sam, you got to get rid of this stuff before they show up and kick you out! Let her take the damn television. It doesn't work anyway.

SAM. That's not the point.

FOSTER. She get that new job?

SAM. Oh. I don't think she knows yet.

(*Bothered.*) Bubble wrap. "In the car." I don't want to get rid of that. My father gave me that when he died.

(**SAM** *is worried.*)

FOSTER. This is what he left you? A TV that doesn't work?

SAM. I got all his stuff. Nobody wanted any of it. I got his teeth, his teeth are in this room somewhere. He had a bunch of money in there, too, you know back in the sixties they had these things called Savings Bonds. You give the government twenty bucks and in like I don't know thirty years it's worth a thousand dollars.

FOSTER. Yeah you told me about the savings bonds a while ago, never heard about the TV. Or the teeth.

If she's going to start moving things along, you got to go through it, Sam. It's all this stuff?

(He goes to look at the pile of papers and folders while **AMELIA** *reenters.)*

AMELIA. You know, Dad, if you want me to take some of these piles of magazines I can do that too, today. We can just put a couple of boxes together while we're at it, maybe.

(She notices that the television is gone from where it was. Reacts with a slow burn.)

SAM. Thanks honey but you know Foster was just saying, you know, I need to go through this stuff. Like some of these papers, I might need that.

AMELIA. Mr. Foster. You didn't say that. Did you say that?

FOSTER. He said he might have some valuable papers in here.

AMELIA. He says that about everything! Ugh.

(Frustrated.) Sorry. Sorry. I was gone for such a short second.

SAM. I am doing it. You want me to do it.

AMELIA. It's not what I want, it's what you have to do.

SAM. Just give me a minute.

AMELIA. You don't have a minute! You have run out of minutes!

(She takes a breath. Bothered, **SAM** *wanders away from her, looking through the things in the room.)*

SAM. Things are more important than they look. Like see this? You'd probably just throw this in a garbage bag.

*(***SAM*** *pulls out a broken guitar.)*

AMELIA. You're absolutely right, give it to me, and I will do that for you.

SAM. And you know what? You'd be throwing away an important artifact. You know whose guitar this is? You know who played this guitar?

AMELIA. Elvis?

SAM. No.

AMELIA. Prince?

SAM. No.

AMELIA. Eric Clapton?

SAM. No.

AMELIA. Willie Nelson.

SAM. Foster, you guess.

FOSTER. I don't know the music world.

SAM. You "don't know the music world"?

FOSTER. That's what I said.

SAM. That's like saying, "I've never been in love."

FOSTER. It is not like saying that!

AMELIA. Who is it, Dad? Is it an actual human being?

SAM. Just give me a minute. I need to talk to him about this.

FOSTER. I don't like music. I don't apologize for that. You listen to music now? It's like noise. You can't, it doesn't sound like anything.

SAM. Okay. Okay. I'll give you that.

AMELIA. Oh my god.

SAM. What?

AMELIA. We were so close to getting something done.

SAM. We're still getting something done. It's just a different thing.

AMELIA. You are two old men talking about how the music kids listen to sucks! That is not doing anything. They were having this same conversation when The Beatles showed up!

SAM. *(To* **FOSTER.***) You* never listened to music? Even when it wasn't noise? Really? Because, that's hard to believe.

AMELIA. Dad.

SAM. What? It's hard to believe.

FOSTER. Sam, we all got our things. My thing is plants. Your thing is this.

> *(He gestures to the piles of paper and garbage.)*

SAM. This isn't a thing.

FOSTER. It's totally a thing. I don't judge it.

SAM. Why would you judge it?

FOSTER. Because it's weird.

SAM. What's weird about it? This is what I'm trying to say!

(Off the guitar.) A lot of people would throw this away, but one man's trash is another man's treasure. One time I read a story in one of these magazines right here, a great story, and it was about actual garbage, piles and piles of garbage. And then little kids were crawling all over it. Looking for something. Like there was something in those piles of garbage.

FOSTER. You mean there was treasure in there?

SAM. Yeah.

AMELIA. No no. There was no treasure there. There are people all over the world who are so poor they have to pick through piles of garbage because they are so poor! It's the problem of living on this planet! It's the disease of capitalism!

SAM. Here she goes.

AMELIA. The corporations just keep making more and more stuff and then it turns into garbage and then the poor people of the earth are just left in piles of garbage and that does not have to be anyone's fate, you don't need to drown in stuff, your life is not supposed to be just about all the JUNK, it's about, it's about…

SAM. Okay I wasn't saying that I have no sympathy for poor children around the world

AMELIA. It sounded like you were saying that –

SAM. I wasn't saying that!

AMELIA. Yeah well that's what it sounds like.

SAM. Well let me come up with a different example.

AMELIA. I don't need any more examples, I understand your point and it's not a good point.

(**FOSTER** *interrupts this.*)

FOSTER. So who played that guitar.

SAM. Okay. So, I knew this guy in the army. They had me at Fort Bragg, they didn't want me fighting overseas. Flat feet. I was a glorified file clerk which was boring but better than getting shot at. And then after four years of that they paid for my college. I never got shot at but I still got the deal. Anyway there was this guy, Seward Remington, Black guy, he worked in this office with me for about six months.

FOSTER. He was also a file clerk?

SAM. He wasn't much for filing. He had been in Viet Nam, he saw some things that left him without all of his common sense, if you know what I mean. Not a bad guy but you wouldn't want him filing anything. He was not fully reliable in that area.

FOSTER. So what did he do?

SAM. General janitorial stuff. Clean the floors, clean the toilets. He didn't say much, but he'd show up at the headquarters every day, very reliable, and he would wear this thing. Across his back. Like a rock and roll star.

FOSTER. They let him do that?

SAM. He was a heroic guy. He had a distinguished service medal, most people don't know what that is, but it's a very big deal. You get it for saving a lot of lives. But he got spooked, apparently, that's what the story was, he couldn't go out there and shoot people up anymore, so he wasn't any use to them over there. At the same time, they didn't want to just kick him out of the Army because of his heroism. It was easy work, is I think what the thinking was. He didn't say much. Just always had this guitar on his back. So I asked him one day, "What's with the guitar?" And he said it belonged to some rock and roller I never heard of, the guy lived on his family's farm in North Carolina off and on, he played guitar in the back of the house and helped with the chickens and such in exchange for a place to stay.

Then he finally moved on, and he told Remington he could keep the guitar, it was busted up anyway. Signed his name on the back.

FOSTER. Who's this guy?

SAM. Seward Remington. Cool name, huh? It was a sad story. Shot himself in the head one day. They sent me over to the barracks to clean out his stuff, which there wasn't much of. I had to call his mom to find out where she wanted me to send it, and she was just sick with grief. She hadn't seen him in a month, and she was just right up the road just twenty minutes away, but families were not allowed to visit the base at that time. I told her that I liked Seward a lot, how we worked together for just a little while but I had a lot of respect for the guy, everybody did. And she said, who? And I said, Seward.

And she said, his name was Sonny. His family that's what they called him. His whole life. That just killed me. Nobody in that office called him that. Anyway. I told her they were going to send her the medals and she didn't want them, she didn't want anything. She was so ripped up. She just hung up on me.

(There is a pause.)

FOSTER. That is the saddest damn story I ever heard.

SAM. I know.

FOSTER. That poor woman. They wouldn't let him go home to her? Her son needed her. She loved him.

SAM. She did.

FOSTER. A white boy with medals would have been allowed to go home to his momma.

SAM. Well.

FOSTER. A white boy would have come home and had his college paid for!

SAM. Wait wait, is this a racial thing?

FOSTER. You bet it's a racial thing. You could have done more for that boy. You didn't even know his name.

SAM. They didn't tell me his nickname.

FOSTER. If he was a white boy, you would have known his name.

SAM. I liked him! I talked to him. He was a sweet guy. He showed me his guitar, I saved it for him. They would have thrown it away.

FOSTER. He should've been home with his mother! He should have been with the people who loved him who saw him.

SAM. Look, don't get mad at me. I did what I could.

FOSTER. I am mad at you. I'm mad at you. My son did two stints in the marines, they actually sent him overseas, worst time of my life. I told him not to go. He came back thank god but he still wakes up with nightmares. He's still not all right all the time. His wife and his boys worried all the time.

SAM. Yeah, it's what happens to them over there.

FOSTER. He's fine! He's FINE, he works at being fine and it is work but you know you got to connect or he could just go someplace else in his head and it's terrible to watch when that happens, what his brain puts him through.

AMELIA. That sounds hard.

FOSTER. And then she's here! Your daughter coming over here all the time, trying to be a good daughter to you to help you get your shit together. To take care of you. And you don't, you don't –

SAM. I don't what?

FOSTER. You don't appreciate her.

AMELIA. He does.

FOSTER. He hides.

SAM. I don't hide.

AMELIA. Okay. That's not what I'm saying.

FOSTER. It's true though.

AMELIA. I just want –

FOSTER. I know what you want. You want to connect.

AMELIA. Actually I want him to clean his house up.

FOSTER. You want to connect with this old fool, and he's more connected to his garbage than he is to you.

AMELIA. That's not –

FOSTER. It is exactly what he is doing

SAM. It is not what I do! Everyone's yelling at me today.

FOSTER. Because you don't connect to anything! There's a whole world out there and you never even walk out that door anymore.

SAM. There's nothing out there

FOSTER. There's a yard. You have a whole yard. And people. Neighbors!

SAM. They called the fire department on me!

FOSTER. They're worried about you!

SAM. Worried about their property values you mean

FOSTER. How do you know? You never talk to them.

SAM. They called the fire department on me!

FOSTER. They should! This place is a hellhole!

SAM. Why are you yelling at me?

FOSTER. Because you sit in garbage while your life circles the drain. And she lets you.

AMELIA. I'm not letting him.

FOSTER. You could do more. This is a desperate situation! You could take responsibility, you could just call a moving company and make this happen.

AMELIA. Like I said, I don't think this is about me.

FOSTER. Everything is about all of us. That woman lost her son before his time, he was a hero, he was a lost soul, you think of all the time they did not have together, she didn't even want his damn medals, you tell me a story like that and you expect me to help you waste the rest of the life that God has given to you, you –

SAM. I understand; I understand what you're saying. I do.

(Pause.)

SAM. Just let me play the record. I got it right here.

> *(After a moment, **SAM** goes to another corner of the pile and pulls out an old record player.)*

> *(**FOSTER** stands there for a moment, looks around at all the junk.)*

FOSTER. You're not listening to me.

SAM. I'm trying to show you something, even though you're not much for music, I think you're going to connect to him.

FOSTER. I'm going.

SAM. It's the end of the story. About Seward. Sonny. You have to know there's a reason I told that story. About Sonny and the guitar. You got to let me get to the end of it.

FOSTER. I'm telling you I'm going!

> *(He starts for the door. **AMELIA** protests, and so does **SAM**.)*

AMELIA. *(Protesting.)* Oh Mr. Foster please don't go he didn't mean what he said

SAM. *(Overlap.)* You can't go until the hear the song, the whole point is

FOSTER. *(Overlap.)* He's not even listening to anything I'm saying.

SAM. *(Overlap.)* That the guy who gave him the guitar could really play that thing and it looks like junk but

FOSTER. *(Overlap.)* I'm going, he's not hearing a word I'm telling him

AMELIA. *(Overlap.)* No no no he didn't mean it

(**SAM** *drops the needle on the record. The first chords of a resounding electric guitar lick come up.* It is a gorgeous sound. It freezes* **FOSTER** *in his tracks.* **SAM** *and* **FOSTER** *and* **AMELIA** *listen for a moment, then* **FOSTER** *splits.* **AMELIA** *follows him.*)

(*In his own world,* **SAM** *mimes playing the guitar. Lights change.*)

---

* A license to produce *I Need That* does not include a performance license for any third-party or copyrighted music. Licensees should create an original composition or use music in the public domain. For further information, please see the Music and Third-Party Materials Use Note on page iii.

Scene Four

(Night. Sam is alone. He puts the guitar away and considers his solitude. Remembers something, goes to a bookshelf and looks up. After a moment, he finds a step stool and climbs it. At the top, he reaches over and removes a large box: It is an old boardgame. Wobbly, he climbs down, sets it on the couch, and climbs back up. Retrieves another boardgame, and carries it down. This time was a little too wobbly as well, but Sam is on a mission. He goes back up the step stool and reaches even further back to grab another boardgame.)

(It falls and he falls as well. In the dark there is the sound of a dangerous crash. Blackout.)

Scene Five

*(Knocking at the door. Then a key, turning in the lock. **AMELIA** steps in. She carries a bag of stuff.)*

AMELIA. *(Calling.)* Dad? Hey, Dad it's me. I just came over for a minute before work because...Dad?

*(She looks around, then sees **SAM** on the floor.)*

AMELIA. Oh my god, Dad?

SAM. I'm fine, just fell asleep down here.

AMELIA. Did you fall?

SAM. No. I didn't fall. No.

(She helps him up.)

What time is it?

AMELIA. Don't lie to me.

SAM. Honey, I wouldn't dream of it. Just like I said, I decided to sleep down here. You're here early.

AMELIA. You fell!

SAM. I did not fall.

AMELIA. You have a bump on your head.

SAM. This? I've had this bump since I was ten years old.

AMELIA. You could have a concussion.

(She goes to the kitchen to get a bag of peas.)

Are you dizzy? You fell and then you fell asleep do you understand how dangerous that is?

(She returns with the peas.)

AMELIA. Just put this on your head.

SAM. I don't need peas.

AMELIA. Just do it.

SAM. What are you doing here?

AMELIA. I had to come before work.

SAM. Oh, you got that job?

AMELIA. I'm still at the old job for now. Well, this doesn't look too bad but I probably should take you to the hospital now.

SAM. I'm not going to the hospital.

AMELIA. You fell Dad!

SAM. I'm spry. I'm a man half my age. I'm not going to any hospital. You want some coffee? Or some cereal? I got a four-day-old plum in here.

AMELIA. No, thanks. I just wanted to drop this off for you.

SAM. Well, don't just leave all that wrapping anywhere. I mean, I don't like it when people come and throw garbage around.

AMELIA. It's a phone.

SAM. A phone? I don't need a phone. I have a landline.

AMELIA. You never pick up. You have the ringer off.

SAM. All those telemarketers, that's the only people who call that number, or a politician.

AMELIA. Which is why you need a cell phone. The only time I ever hear from you is when Mr. Foster is here, because he lets you use his phone.

SAM. I like to use Foster's phone. That seems to be working.

AMELIA. Well, you're not going to be able to do that anymore.

SAM. Why not?

AMELIA. Because he's leaving.

SAM. Leaving?

AMELIA. Yes, he called me and said he's moving away.

SAM. He didn't say that.

AMELIA. He did, Dad, he's moving away. Mr. Foster is moving.

SAM. You misunderstood him.

AMELIA. *(Snapping.)* I did not misunderstand. He was very clear. He is giving up his apartment and moving somewhere else, he didn't say where.

SAM. He called you? Why didn't he call me?

AMELIA. Because he couldn't get hold of you because you don't answer your landline!

SAM. Well, why didn't he just come over?

AMELIA. I don't know. You can call him and ask him. Here. The on/off button is on the side.

(She shows him how.)

SAM. I know how to use a phone.

(He moves away from her.)

AMELIA. I can't believe he's just announcing this and doing it. I mean, he's like doing it right away, apparently, and what is supposed to happen to you, if he's not here.

SAM. I'm fine.

AMELIA. You're not fine, Dad! You need to clean this place up and you don't answer your landline and you can't even leave the stupid house.

SAM. I can leave the house! I don't want to leave the house!

AMELIA. Oh god. He was right, Mr. Foster was right. I should have taken care of this, I should have hired movers and just forced you.

SAM. Forced me? Force!

AMELIA. DAD.

SAM. I'm an independent human being. Very spry as you just saw. I fell as you just saw and almost broke my neck! And then I popped right back up. No one is taking over my life. Not you, not anybody. This is my home, my space, my stuff. I choose. Not you. Not Foster. Nobody. This is America.

AMELIA. You're not hearing me, you're not taking things in.

SAM. I'm not taking things in because you told me I got to be throwing things out! Make up your mind.

AMELIA. Dad, come on! This isn't working. Everything just gets worse. Every time I come over here it's worse.

SAM. Then don't come.

AMELIA. *(Mean.)* If Mr. Foster doesn't come, and then I don't come, who are you going to talk to?

SAM. I'll talk to the firemen, you tell me they're coming any minute.

AMELIA. Yeah, yeah, okay; you can talk to them.

Look at this place. Old magazines no one reads. Clothes no one wears. Board games no one plays. But you keep them because they remind you of all those brothers and sisters who were always horrible to you. Seven of them, all good Catholics, and none of them came to Mom's funeral. You remember that, right?

SAM. Half of them are dead.

AMELIA. None of them call you.

SAM. I don't need to talk to dead people on the phone.

AMELIA. Then why are you holding onto the stupid games you played with them! This is junk, nobody uses it, and if you would throw it out it wouldn't take up space in your house or your brain which would be a good thing because your useless family doesn't deserve to be remembered!

SAM. Your mom loved these. We played them when you were a kid. Clue. She always remembered how much you liked that one. It was one of the last things she remembered. One day she just started talking about it and I let her hold the card and she remembered Mrs. White, in the conservatory, with the lead pipe.

AMELIA. Mrs. White!

(He hands her the cards, shows her.)

SAM. Lead pipe. Conservatory. Here's another one she liked. Sorry.

AMELIA. Sorry. I remember.

SAM. You loved this game.

AMELIA. I didn't love it.

SAM. You did! You always wanted to play. You liked all the tricks the cards do.

AMELIA. Going backwards with the four.

SAM. That's right.

AMELIA. "Sorry!"

SAM. You used to get so mad when you got sent back home.

AMELIA. That's why I didn't like it! It's mean!

SAM. Except when you got to do it to someone else! Although your mother really never liked that part.

AMELIA. I remember.

(This is a good memory.)

SAM. She would hide it in the deck and pick another card. I was like, what's the point? The Sorry card is the point.

AMELIA. I remember.

SAM. You want to take these things?

(He gestures to the board games.)

AMELIA. What? Really?

SAM. Sure. You're right. I don't need to save all this. Take it.

AMELIA. Okay. I'll just put them back in this green tub here.

(She starts to do this.)

SAM. Maybe, maybe leave the Monopoly. That was a fun game. Those little pieces, the shoe and the hat. My favorite one was the hat.

(She looks at him.)

You should probably leave Sorry.

AMELIA. Dad. They will do it. I've already called to beg them for a little more time and... And then, it's just, the fact is, all your stuff would be just gone. Save something. And let other things go. Please.

(A pause.)

SAM. Go ahead and take all of it. I don't care. Take everything. You're right. I don't need this stuff. You should bring a truck like tomorrow, or the next day, just pull it up to the door and we'll throw everything out the window since that's so important to you. It's all anyone can talk about anymore, stuff, throw your stuff away. You know a lot of people have stuff. Everyone has stuff! But obviously there's a lot of rules about it. Got to make sure, even if it's your own house, got to follow the rules. Take everything. Take the magazines. Take the dishes. Take all the board games, it doesn't matter that maybe some night when I'm here all alone I might just want to look at one or two, that's nothing. Take it all! No wait wait. Can I maybe just keep one chair? A chair, in the middle of an empty room. Is that okay? A chair and plate and a cup. Maybe a fork. If someone brings me a taco someday. I could have a chair and a plate and a fork and eat my taco. Oh and one other thing. A cushion. Could I have a cushion, for my chair? Is that too much, is that too much?

(They stand and consider each other. **AMELIA** *goes. Lights fade.)*

Scene Six

(**SAM** *alone on the couch. He is playing Sorry, by himself. He picks up a card.*)

SAM. Eight. Screw you, eight. I can't do anything with an eight, I got no one on the board.

(*Picks up another card.*)

Yes! Thank you number two but where were you a second ago when red needed you?

(*As yellow.*) Tough luck, red. I get another card... another eight!

(*He moves his yellow piece. Picks up another card.*)

Seven for blue! Very good. We will move four then slide.

(*He does.*)

And over here you get to move three then slide. Very promising moment for the blue team. Green, what do you have up your sleeve?

(*He picks up a card.*)

Five. Boring but what are you going to do, it's better than sitting home.

(*He picks up another card.*)

(*As red.*) Aw come on. I'm having a terrible time.

(*Another card.*)

And that's a four for yellow. Backward four. What's up for blue.

(*He picks up a card, and moves blue. He picks up another card.*)

Oh yes. Two! Blue keeps charging ahead. This is excellent. I love a game where everything just goes your way. Like the cards are magic, god just shuffled them in place so that every time I pick one, it's something that works. Not that you want to get cocky, you can't...

(Another card. It's SORRY.)

Red. Oh yeah red! Sorry! You see that, blue? Fuck you. Sooooorrrrry. You're back at start and I'm on the board.

(Another card.)

Yellow, I got nothing to say.

(As yellow.) I know, I know. Some games you just have to just make it through and hope that you can be the tortoise, nobody notices you but you're just calmly making it around the...

(Another card.)

(As blue.) SORRY. SORRY, who are we going for, who...

(As yellow.) I just got kicked back home by red.

(As red.) Well green will get you closer.

(As green.) We're nowhere close! We're barely getting started. We don't do you any good at all. It's not even worth it swapping out with us. You might as well stay in start. You can't go for one of us.

(As blue.) Yeah, I'm not interested in you guys.

(As red.) Well you can't, come on I'm barely on the board! What's the point of going after me?

(As blue, evil delight.) Sorryyyyyy.

(As red.) Come on.

(As blue.) You started this.

(Red.) You'd have all your pieces out!

(Yellow.) Come on guys it's a game.

(Red.) It's so not fair.

(Blue.) Sorrryyyy

(Red.) Stop saying that. You'd have three out, I'd have none. It's not fair.

(Blue.) This isn't about what's fair, it's about winning. Winning.

(Red.) I'M LOSING.

(Yellow.) Whose turn is it?

(Blue.) Sorry. Sorrry! Sorry! SORRY.

(Red.) Come on Pauly, you can't do that Pauly.

(Blue.) Sammy you suck, you sorry Sammy, you SUCK

> *(He does a little dance as blue, making the move, kicking red back home.)*

(As red.) Stop it! It isn't funny! I hate this game. It isn't fair!

> *(**SAM** throws the board against the wall. There is a moment of silence. He starts to cry. After a long moment he looks around. He stands and looks around. He sees that he's alone. He touches the wall. He finds the phone. Looks around. Doesn't know what to do. After a moment, he goes to the pile of boxes of garbage bags and starts to clean up.)*

> *(Lights fade.)*

Scene Seven

(**FOSTER** *is standing there watching* **SAM** *clean. Big full garbage bags stand by the door.)*

FOSTER. What are you doing?

SAM. I'm cleaning up.

FOSTER. Why?

SAM. What do you mean why? You don't think it's time to clean up?

FOSTER. It's hard to even answer that. You been living like this for...

SAM. Well, I got tired of listening to everyone yell at me. I'm cleaning up.

FOSTER. Then what are you gonna to do?

SAM. You know I didn't invite you here. You came over here. Why'd you come over here?

FOSTER. I brought you some... Just a hamburger.

SAM. You can put it over there.

FOSTER. You're not hungry?

SAM. I got food coming.

FOSTER. You got food coming.

SAM. Yes. I called the place, on the phone, you give them a credit card number and they bring it to you.

FOSTER. I'm aware of this service.

SAM. Good.

(*He keeps cleaning.)*

FOSTER. Are you mad at me?

SAM. Why would I be mad at you?

FOSTER. I can think of a few reasons.

SAM. Well, I'm not mad. The other day, when you expressed your frustration, because I was not as sensitive as I maybe should have been about the story of my fellow man, who was suffering, I can see why that made you angry. So I get it. And I'm not mad.

FOSTER. That's not what you might be mad about.

SAM. Oh there are other things?

FOSTER. Yeah.

SAM. Like what?

FOSTER. Like I been stealing from you.

> *(That stops* **SAM** *in his tracks. He looks at him.)*

SAM. You been stealing from me?

FOSTER. You got a lot of valuable stuff here, Sam. You wouldn't know it to look at it.

SAM. I would know. It's what I've been saying. All of this is treasure.

FOSTER. No, all of this is junk. I'm not going to say garbage because I know that's offensive to you. But this is all junk. It's just every now and then a piece of junk is worth money. Over time you tell me a story or two, I could figure out what piece of junk was worth something and just take it.

SAM. Just take it.

FOSTER. Not just take it. Wait for you to turn around or go to the bathroom. And then I'd just take it. I listen to your stories, I love your stories, but here's a story for you. I been living over there in that little place back of Mrs. Gunderson's how long, she's a nightmare, you know about this. Now she got her son showing up half the time to bug me, I'm a couple days late they're slipping notes under my door.

They want to sell, and if I'm still there it makes it harder, or they can't make as much money, who knows what all they're up to. But I'm not kidding. Just a few days late, and that happens more and more because the mail is a mess, my social security or my shitty little pension don't come on time and they're out there ready to kick me out. Last three months the checks didn't come at all, and they went to the sheriff's office and I got an official eviction notice. I think the son went through my mail and took those checks in all honesty; I think he's got them stashed somewhere. I called the social security and the bank, to get them to replace the money and I been filling out forms like you don't want to know and it just takes forever, who knows when that money's going to show up. And I don't want to bother my kids with this stuff; they don't want me living on my own anymore but I swear it's my place. You know, it's my place, it ain't much but I live there and I want to stay there. You understand that. I don't like asking for help. You ask for help, the world the way it is now, they give you help and then they come after you. And this isn't the first time. Some months I'd be really strapped and you just sitting here with this stuff, you don't even know if you have it or not. So I took it. Just last week I took that ring that lady gave you from the bingo down to the pawn shop on seventh. You know how much that was worth? Two thousand dollars. And I went and cashed in those savings bonds, too. That was worth six hundred.

(**SAM** *starts toward the box of bingo stuff, but Foster stops him.*)

It's not there, Sam because I took it and you didn't even notice it was gone.

FOSTER. I took some of your magazines, too. You think to look at them, those things can't be worth shit, but I went and looked on Ebay, what people are buying and selling. So when you were taking a shower one day I sat out here and went through like three piles of magazines and took six or seven. And then on Ebay, I made like, seventeen hundred dollars.

(*Then.*)

That's Link Wray's old guitar. I started to, I mean I didn't finish because I just, it's probably worth... He signed it. Link Wray signed it for that poor boy who he gave it to, and now it's worth a lot. And I was thinking about stealing that guitar from you. I was figuring the whole thing out. How I'd do it. Wait for you to go in the shower. The things I can get up to, while you're in the shower! I had the whole thing planned out. I was thinking about how I'd rearrange your pile of junk over here first, so you wouldn't miss it for quite a while. The whole thing, I knew how to do it, I was gonna do it... And I was so ashamed. I mean, really just...this is all too much. It's too much.

(*Choking up.*) I'm a thief. I'm a fucking thief. I did that to myself because I didn't want to live on someone else's pity.

SAM. No no no no stop man. Listen. I knew this was happening. All along. And I was not going to just let you steal my guitar. So you don't have to worry about that.

FOSTER. Bullshit. Don't talk to me like I'm a fool. I'm an old man is what I am, and I have too much pride. That's what your problem is, Sam, you just –. No. I'm not here to tell you what your problem is. I'm here to tell you I'm sorry. I could've just left and not told you any of this but I wanted things to be honest between us. I took your stuff. And I'm sorry.

(There's a knock at the door. Beat. Another knock.)

*(**SAM** suddenly starts barking, like a dog. He goes to the window, barking. The person on the porch bolts. **FOSTER** starts to laugh. **SAM** turns to include him, delighted.)*

SAM. I was trying to scare off the firemen. It's not the firemen. It's the food!

*(**FOSTER** goes to open the door and fetch the food.)*

FOSTER. It's so weird that they do that now. Just leave the food. You don't even see the guy, the food is just there. Everybody in their own little caves. He's not in a cave, he's just on a bike riding around out there. It didn't use to be like this. Well, you know that.

(Then.)

This is going to get cold if you don't eat it.

SAM. You want some?

FOSTER. What is it?

SAM. Chinese food.

FOSTER. From the place down there on the corner of Third and Union?

SAM. I guess.

FOSTER. You get the chicken with the peanuts and the red peppers?

SAM. Yeah, I got that and the pork dumplings and some broccoli.

FOSTER. You got broccoli?

SAM. You know, vegetables are, we should continue to eat vegetables even into the twilight of our lives.

FOSTER. Twilight of our lives.

SAM. Yeah.

(*They think about that.*)

FOSTER. Maybe I'll have the hamburger.

SAM. Okay. I'll get some plates.

(**SAM** *goes and gets some plates.*)

FOSTER. I'm moving, Sam. I know Amelia already told you. I was afraid to tell you.

(**SAM** *stops.*)

My son found a place in his building, it's a little smaller but if I need help he and his wife can just come up a couple floors, I'll be right there. If I have a problem with my checks coming on time, they can help me figure it out. I never wanted to live in a big apartment building like that but he makes a lot of sense. It's in Cleveland.

SAM. What floor?

FOSTER. It's the eleventh floor, I'd be all the way up there on the eleventh floor, it's a pretty big building.

SAM. But no garden.

FOSTER. Eleventh floor, no, you don't get the garden. He says there's a couple of nice windows. I can have some house plants.

(*This is sobering news.*)

SAM. That is unacceptable.

FOSTER. It's not, necessarily. I been looking through some stuff on the internet.

SAM. The internet.

FOSTER. Yes, you've heard of it. They have pictures of people with plants in their houses.

SAM. Inside.

FOSTER. Sam you say that as if you ever go outside which you do not.

SAM. The eleventh floor.

FOSTER. It'll be fine. Might be nice to live up in the air instead of down on the ground.

SAM. It doesn't sound nice. It does not sound nice at all. People don't belong in the air. This is why it took them so long to figure out how to fly.

FOSTER. Well, I'm going to fly. I'm going to put myself on an airplane and fly to Cleveland.

SAM. Cleveland is…who wants to live in Cleveland.

FOSTER. I've heard nice things about Cleveland. There's a lake there. Supposed to be nice.

SAM. Cleveland? *CLEVELAND*. It doesn't sound good. It just doesn't. Where is Cleveland?

FOSTER. You know where Cleveland is. It's in Ohio.

SAM. *OHIO?* OHIO? Oh god. Oh god.

FOSTER. Ohio is fine.

SAM. Ohio is the source of all disappointment and grief in America.

FOSTER. Now you know that's crazy and you are not a crazy person, Sam. No matter what you let people think. I know you. You're my best friend. Even though I been stealing from you.

(*Then.*)

I HAVE been stealing from you, and you are my best friend, and you forgive me. Without even thinking twice. You are not crazy. You are a kind man. Your wife died for a long time and you stood by her side while she just disappeared, I watched you do it, and it left you in this place

SAM. I'm fine in this place.

FOSTER. You are not fine my friend. This isn't fine. You're too alone.

SAM. Then don't go. Stay here. I mean it, stay here. Here! With me.

FOSTER. Sam, there's barely room for you here.

SAM. We could figure something out. I got a front yard, a backyard.

FOSTER. That is not a backyard.

SAM. There's a lot of room back there.

FOSTER. That you filled with junk. That old Chrysler, how long that been sitting back there.

SAM. You get rid of it. We get rid of it and you can have a garden.

FOSTER. It's concrete under it! That's a carport back there.

SAM. No listen, we jackhammer that stuff up.

FOSTER. You and me. In the twilight of our lives we're going to get us a jackhammer.

> *(They laugh together.)*

SAM. This isn't twilight! You're giving up too soon.

FOSTER. We're old.

SAM. We're not old! I'm spry.

FOSTER. You can't even haul away a bag of magazines!

SAM. I've been doing it. I started last night. Look at these bags. You can't not have noticed.

FOSTER. Sam. You're never going to get rid of this stuff.

SAM. No no, I am, I'm doing it.

I've been meaning to do this. I've been talking about it forever. And I've been organizing, but you know what? I'm done with organizing. Aren't you going to help me?

FOSTER. I'm eating.

SAM. Oh sorry. Of course, you finish eating. Take your time. I'm just going to get this going, though.

(*He starts to move a lot of things toward the door.* **FOSTER** *watches him.*)

FOSTER. You think that's going to make that lady across the street like you any better?

SAM. I don't care about her. It just kind of feels good.

FOSTER. Go outside, walk down the steps, go around back and put it in the garbage can. I bet that feels good too.

SAM. I'll get to that. First we got to get this stuff out of here, so we both can have more of a sense of how big this place is. I mean, I just don't see flying to Cleveland as a great idea when there's someplace better right around the corner from where you're living now.

(**FOSTER** *nods, sets his plate down somewhere.*)

FOSTER. Sam I don't think you should get too excited by this idea.

SAM. Here, we'll get rid of these books over here.

FOSTER. It's a lot of books.

SAM. Ginny, she was always reading.

(*Then.*)

And then, when she got sick, it helped her to have her books...stuff. It helped her remember who she was.

SAM. And of course that was what you wanted. Every day. Keep her with you. Keep her stuff around her. Keep her books! Keep her...keep...

> *(A beat. He has a book in his hand.)*

> *(**SAM** rips the book in half. Then he rips it some more.)*

FOSTER. Sam, Sam come on. Sam.

SAM. There's nothing, this book is nothing. We can get rid of all this stuff. It's all nothing.

> *(He starts to throw things out. He throws books out the door. He throws anything he can lay his hands on, out the door.)*

Are you going to help me or not?

> *(After a moment, **FOSTER** goes to his side, takes a book from him. He rips it in half. Then he throws both halves out the door.)*

FOSTER. Let's do this.

> *(**SAM** and **FOSTER** start moving piles of books, games, dishes, magazines, whatever they can lay their hands on. **FOSTER** manages to get bags and boxes and crates out the door, onto the porch. **SAM** just moves things out back, through the kitchen. He still cannot face the outside world, but he doesn't have to for now. The two **MEN** just keep cleaning and music rises and supports them.* After a good long process, which is both a scene*

---

* A license to produce *I Need That* does not include a performance license for any third-party or copyrighted music. Licensees should create an original composition or use music in the public domain. For further information, please see the Music and Third-Party Materials Use Note on page iii

change and a night of feverish cleaning, they collapse. They haven't solved everything, but they have made serious progress.)

Scene Eight

*(Morning. **SAM** and **FOSTER**, passed out. The door and windows are open, a golden light suffuses the room.)*

*(**AMELIA** enters. Before she comes in, she stands out on the porch, looking at the lawn, which is now full of junk. She steps inside and looks around, astonished.)*

AMELIA. Oh my god.

*(She sees the sleeping **MEN**. She steps in for a moment, looks around. It takes her a minute to get it. The place is a completely different place. It's not necessarily clean. It is more empty.)*

*(She starts to cry. For a moment she cries, silently, then more so. The **MEN** stir. **FOSTER** wakes first. He sees **AMELIA** there, crying, sits up.)*

FOSTER. Sam. Sam. Wake up. Amelia's here.

SAM. Amelia?

(He gets up, hurries over to her.)

Amelia. I didn't know you were coming over today. It's good to see you.

(She hugs him. He hugs her back.)

AMELIA. The place looks great, Dad.

SAM. It's just a beginning. I'm still organizing some stuff. The yard could use a little work.

AMELIA. No question. We will definitely have to get to that. But I think you've made real progress.

(She laughs and goes and sits on the couch.)

Look at this! You can sit on the couch without moving anything. I used to love this couch. Remember when we had to get it recovered because the arms were just worn to bits so Mom took me with her to the fabric store and we looked and looked and then she found this incredible blue velvet and the man in the store kept telling her it would stain and it would be hard to clean and the color was too light but she said it would look like the sky. And that's why we always had so many throws on it because they kept it…

> *(She takes the throws off as she talks and the couch underneath reveals itself as a beautiful silver blue.)*

FOSTER. That couch been under there the whole time?

AMELIA. *(Happy.)* You had to keep it covered with all the blankets, to keep it nice.

FOSTER. Yeah, well. It worked.

AMELIA. Isn't it pretty?

FOSTER. It's real nice.

SAM. You want some breakfast? Cereal? Eggs? Let me get some coffee going.

> *(He heads for the kitchen.)*

FOSTER. I got to go, Sam. I'm flying out this afternoon.

> *(There is a moment of silence at that.)*

SAM. I thought you were going to stay here.

FOSTER. I told you not to get too excited about that. It's not just for me. It's for my son, too. He needs me. He needs his dad.

*(To **AMELIA**.)* I'm going to Cleveland.

AMELIA. Oh, I hear Cleveland's nice.

FOSTER. My son found a place for me in his own building there.

AMELIA. How many kids does he have now?

FOSTER. Three little boys.

AMELIA. So you'll get to see your grandkids all the time.

FOSTER. So it seems.

AMELIA. You'll get to live in a whole new city!

FOSTER. I'm thinking that too.

AMELIA. That's really great. A whole new city.

SAM. In OHIO.

AMELIA. There's a lake there, on the other side is Canada. Maybe you'll get to go to Canada.

FOSTER. Maybe.

SAM. Well isn't that nice. Isn't that cozy. Isn't that just wonderful. Life moves on.

(There is a silence at that.)

FOSTER. I'm going to say goodbye then.

SAM. WAIT.

(A pause.)

You've been a good friend.

FOSTER. You too, Sam.

SAM. I want to give you something.

FOSTER. That's not necessary.

SAM. All this stuff, you don't want something to remember me to by? Here. Here. Here.

(He pulls the guitar out of the corner.)

FOSTER. I'm not taking that.

SAM. You have to because it's a present.

> *(Then.)*

Don't sell it, okay.

FOSTER. I won't.

SAM. I mean, unless you have to.

FOSTER. I'm not going to sell it, Sam.

SAM. Just wait. Just one more thing. Let me get you a glass of water.

FOSTER. I'm fine Sam.

SAM. *(He nods towards* **AMELIA.***)* Ask her. It's the morning, you need a glass of water to get you going.

> *(He goes into the kitchen, pours a glass of water into a glass, and brings it to* **FOSTER.***)*

Go ahead, drink it. Drink it!

> *(***FOSTER*** does.* **SAM** *is waiting for him to finish.* **FOSTER** *hands the glass back to him.)*

See this glass? Now I can take this glass and put it on top of the coffee table, and every time I see it, I'll think of you.

> *(He goes and puts it on top of the coffee table.* **AMELIA** *and* **FOSTER** *watch him do it.)*

FOSTER. Good.

> *(Then.)*

Goodbye, Amelia.

AMELIA. Goodbye, Mr. Foster.

> *(She reaches up and kisses him goodbye. He heads for the door. Then he comes back, to* **SAM.***)*

(After a moment, the two **MEN** *look at each other and nod, unable to speak.* **FOSTER** *turns and goes out the door.* **SAM** *follows him and watches him go. He waits in the door as long as he can. He turns back to* **AMELIA.** *Looks around.)*

SAM. The place looks weird now. There's like, nothing here.

AMELIA. The couch is here. Mr. Foster's glass. We do have to keep getting rid of the magazines and the piles of clothes –

SAM. Those are your mother's clothes.

(She stops, looks at him.)

Take them, take them.

(She continues packing up stuff. He is distracted, unhappy.)

AMELIA. I'll drive them over to the Goodwill this afternoon. And for sure I have to call Mrs. Wallace across the street so she doesn't freak out. It looks like a garbage truck took a dump on the yard.

(She keeps putting stuff in garbage bags. **SAM** *looks around.)*

SAM. She's gone.

AMELIA. Oh please she's over there. I can feel her hating us through her front windows.

SAM. Not her. Your mother.

AMELIA. Oh.

SAM. She always liked it with the books everywhere. They made her feel safe. All of it. It's not like I never tried. I thought, maybe if there was less stuff, it would make it easier. But then she knew she was missing things and she didn't know what she was missing. She couldn't remember the names of things anymore. Like "lamp" or "chair" or "plug." "Book." I had to put Post-Its on everything. And then she'd make me take them all off whenever you came home from college.

AMELIA. I found one once. It said "Wednesday."

SAM. She was just so embarrassed that she couldn't remember. And then she forgot who I was. She would come up to me and ask me where Sam was. And I'd tell her, I'm here, I'm Sam, and it made her so angry, she meant a different Sam. At some point she decided there were two Sams, there was me, the one she didn't want, and the young Sam, who she couldn't find. She would look all over the house for him. Then she got so mad at me, because I wasn't the Sam she wanted, she tried to stab me with a knife. She did; she came after me with a kitchen knife.

AMELIA. You never told me about that.

SAM. You didn't need to know that stuff. You have a life, you have a job. I never liked my work. Sitting around an office and making phone calls. Some people don't get a job that they love. I never had much of a family, either. But I had you and your mother. And Foster. We've been friends thirty years. He saw your mother get sick. He saw her forget me.

> *(This is hard for him to talk about.)*

And you know, the stupid thing is, I can't really remember her now. The way she was before. All I remember are the Post-Its. And the knife. It's happening to me. What happened to her. She disappeared.

> *(A beat.)*

I don't want to disappear. Do you see? Do you see now? These things, the things you can touch. They keep the world from disappearing. And then you don't disappear.

AMELIA. Dad. You remember everything. In excruciating detail. The level of minutiae in your head

SAM. *(Cutting her off.)* Because of the stuff. Memories don't just live inside us, they all live around us. And all of this is the tuning fork.

(He looks around. Touches a few things.)

AMELIA. Things don't give your life meaning. People do.

SAM. And when they go? Foster's not here. Your mom's not here.

AMELIA. I'm here.

*(**SAM** turns to her.)*

SAM. Can we go?

AMELIA. Go? You mean – outside?

SAM. Yeah.

(He goes to the door, opens it.)

AMELIA. *(Growing hope.)* You want to go outside?

SAM. Yeah, I do. I want to go outside. I want to take a walk.

AMELIA. *(Astonished.)* A walk!

SAM. Yeah. And then I want to go to your place.

AMELIA. My place?

SAM. I've never been to your place. How long have you lived there, and I've never been there.

AMELIA. Okay let's not get ahead of ourselves. A walk sounds good.

SAM. I want to see your apartment. I want to see where you live.

AMELIA. It's not very big.

SAM. I don't care. I want to see your life. You were such a swell little kid. Always showing me your stuff. Your little animals. Those sticker books. You wanted me to look at everything. We'd walk down the street, you'd pick up a rock and say look, Daddy! A rock! Everything was a treasure to you. I want to see what you treasure now. Let's go to your place for once. I'm not saying I'm moving in with you or anything.

AMELIA. Good because you can't.

SAM. And, I don't need to because I have my own house. You get to see my house all the time. I want to see your house.

> (**AMELIA** *is caught. But he is busy, getting his jacket.*)

AMELIA. It's a little messy right now.

SAM. Amelia. You don't have to apologize to me about a messy house. Please.

AMELIA. It's REALLY messy. It's…it's really messy, Dad. I mean, it's like…messy Messy. It's like…messy.

> (*Beat.*)

I saved all my clothes from college, because I liked college and I liked how I looked in them but I never wear them. So my closets are completely useless, they're full of clothes from ten years ago. I have like three outfits that I keep out on hangers in the living room and then every day I shower at the gym and pretend that I'm ultra fit but it's because there's so much stuff in my shower at home, I can't use it. Plus I have too much furniture. I buy it at thrift stores. I see these things and it seems all of them seem like something I have to have, everything I see, I think I need that, but now it's crowded, my own house is so crowded and it feels normal.

SAM. You've been living like me?

AMELIA. Yes.

SAM. *(Sad.)* That's a cage, honey.

AMELIA. I know! It's so crowded, and there are no people. I can't invite friends over. Because I'm embarrassed. I can't date anybody! And every day I think I will clean this up, I will and then I don't do it.

SAM. It should be easy for you. You have so many packing materials.

(There is a sad pause.)

AMELIA. Nobody knows at my work.

SAM. Well, no, if you tell people they try to evict you. Don't tell anybody.

AMELIA. They tried to promote me. I got a promotion, they wanted to send me to Nebraska.

SAM. Nebraska?

AMELIA. It was a good offer. And I was going to take it. I thought, I can walk away from all this JUNK and just start over and I was doing it! But then that stupid Mrs. Wallace and the code board and the fire department. Then Mr. Foster decided to MOVE and if he moves, and you lose your house and I'm not here? What would happen then?

SAM. No. No. No! It's not your responsibility.

AMELIA. Dad. Would you leave me?

SAM. You bet I would.

AMELIA. The way you left Mom?

(There is a sad pause at that.)

SAM. Why didn't you ever tell me any of this?

AMELIA. Oh, Dad. There's so much past here. I didn't know how to fit the present into it.

> (*A beat. He looks out the door. Looks back at her.*)

SAM. Honey, you got to listen to me now. You have to go to Nebraska. That's way better than Ohio. You need to move on. I can take care of this.

AMELIA. Oh sure.

SAM. I'm serious. Nebraska's nice. The Great Plains. Lot of space. You can spread out. And there are nice people there so I hear.

AMELIA. So Ohio sucks but Nebraska is nice.

SAM. Honey, the point is, time keeps coming. And you're a young person. It's one thing for me to stand in the past. But it would kill me if you did that. It would kill me.

> (*He starts to cry a little. She goes to him.*)

AMELIA. Dad –

SAM. No, I mean it. I refuse to have you stay here. I refuse! It's not your job to take care of me! It's my job to take care of you! And I can do this! I've already started! They're not kicking me out of my own house. I'm on top of this. You have to go. I'm serious. Go get on a plane and just go to Nebraska. Leave all that shit in your apartment; just leave it! Do it now. I mean, okay. Okay. I'm going to say this. In general, you don't want to move too fast. Like the future, what's coming? You get to a certain point, you don't want to eat vegetables anymore because vegetables and water, that's a young person's game.

AMELIA. No it's not.

SAM. The point is, they don't know what they're doing anywhere on this planet. Nebraska could be awesome, you should go there, meet someone nice and have kids. That's who you take care of.

AMELIA. You could come with me. We could both just go get on a plane.

(*There is a moment where that seems to be a possibility. He nods, looks around.*)

SAM. Honey. Don't ask for miracles. You're a young woman, you're beautiful, you're so full of life, and you're going to go live. And I'm not going to let you back in. I'm fine. But you have to go.

AMELIA. Can I have the Sorry game?

SAM. Absolutely not.

(*They consider each other. She nods, goes to him, and they hold each other for a long moment. Then, she goes.*)

(*He goes to the door and shuts it.*)

(*He goes and sits on that beautiful couch. He touches it. He takes out the Sorry board. He holds it, then opens it and looks at what's inside.*)

(*He takes out the board, looks around, alone.*)

Sorry.

AMELIA. (*Yelling.*) Dad! Are you coming or not?

SAM. (*To himself.*) Thank god. She needs me! Nobody should go to Nebraska alone.

(*He takes the Sorry board and goes to the door. He opens it. Stares out into the world beyond. For a moment he's not sure he can do it.*)

(*And then he steps out.*)

(*Blackout.*)

End of Play

www.ingramcontent.com/pod-product-compliance
Lightning Source LLC
Chambersburg PA
CBHW072151130726
47909CB00004BB/1581